DOCTOR · WHO

DECIDE YOUR DESTINY

The Spaceship Graveyard

by Colin Brake

EDWARD

DOCTOR·WHO

❀ DECIDE YOUR DESTINY

BBC CHILDREN'S BOOKS
Published by the Penguin Group
Penguin Books Ltd, 80 Strand, London, WC2R 0RL, England
Penguin Group (USA) Inc., 375 Hudson Street, New York, New York 10014, USA
Penguin Books (Australia) Ltd, 250 Camberwell Road, Camberwell, Victoria 3124, Australia.
(A division of Pearson Australia Group Pty Ltd)
Canada, India, New Zealand, South Africa
Published by BBC Children's Books, 2007
Text and design © Children's Character Books, 2007
Written by Colin Brake
10 9 8 7 6 5 4 3 2 1
ISBN-13: 978-1-40590-376-9
ISBN-10: 1-40590-376-7
Printed in Great Britain by Clays Ltd, St Ives plc

The Spaceship
Graveyard

1 | The TARDIS is pitching about like a small rowing boat in
a raging storm. The Doctor has managed to strap you and
Martha into the seat belts attached to the seats mounted near
the central control console but remains unsecured himself.
Somehow, despite the wild ride, the time ship's owner is still
on his feet, skipping around the console, pulling levers and
flicking switches in a desperate dance.

You are beginning to wonder if it was a good idea to
investigate the strange blue box that appeared mysteriously
in your street. Inside you'd found this huge control room and
the Doctor and Martha. The Doctor had taken off before he
realised you were on-board and he offered you a quick trip
in time and space before taking you home — which seemed
like a good idea at the time!

When the turbulence began numerous alarm bells sounded
but now they are silenced leaving the strained groans of the
engines filling the air. Suddenly the lights go out, plunging

you into darkness for a second, before emergency red lighting comes on, making the console room look like a spooky fire-lit cavern.

'What's happening?' Martha asks, trying not to sound scared or too worried.

'I wish I knew,' the Doctor tells her, flashing her a quick reassuring grin, 'but I'm sure it's nothing to worry about.'

At that moment the engines stop completely leaving a deep and frightening silence.

'Oh dear,' mutters the Doctor in a worried tone, 'I may have been wrong about not worrying. Very wrong.'

Desperately he pulls at a series of levers and begins pumping what appears to be a bicycle pump that's connected to the ship by a long rubber tube.

If the engines respond and fire back into activity, go to 63. If nothing happens, go to 79.

2 The robot tells you that he cannot allow that.

'I am programmed to protect the system files from any stranger.'

The Doctor pulls out his sonic screwdriver and fires a blast at the robot, which freezes.

'Sorry,' he tells the now non-functioning robot.

'What have you done?' asks Martha.

'Put him on standby,' says the Doctor, hurrying over to a console, 'I'll turn him back on later.'

'What are you looking for?' you ask.

'I don't really know,' confesses the Doctor, as he rapidly scans the controls, trying to ascertain the functions.

'This device has been operating for thousands of years but it's still operating on its original settings. There must be a more efficient way to use all the energy,' he tells you.

Suddenly you hear heavy footsteps and the aliens you met earlier arrive.

If you call out a warning go to 69. If they fire a warning shot, go to 10.

The Doctor shakes his head.

'That's not the answer,' he says quietly.

The human survivor, who has told you his name is Dylon Kesh, stands his ground.

'We have no choice,' he insists firmly. 'While that machine is operating we cannot leave this planet. But if it is stopped then we can repair our ships and escape.'

'But you heard the Doctor,' you tell him in a shocked tone, 'if the machine stops working it will be a disaster.'

The man looks at you sadly. 'Kid,' he tells you, 'it's a tough universe. Bad things happen. But at the end of the day you have to look after Number One.'

Martha and you take up positions either side of the Time Lord.

The man shakes his head and produces a laser weapon from within his ragged jacket.

If he speaks next, go to 33. If the Doctor speaks next, go to 17.

4 | Suddenly there is an explosion nearby and a pair of doors is blown open. The three battle armour-clad soldiers that you met earlier file into the room, guns aimed and ready, and surround you.

'We want the device that stole our energy,' the leader states bluntly.

'The Shield?'

'Whatever it is called, we want it and we want it now,' the warrior says simply.

You and Martha both step forward.

'You can't just take it,' you begin to say and Martha completes your thought. 'It's the only thing keeping this system from being crushed in a black hole!' she tells them.

During this the Doctor has quietly slipped into the background. Out of the corner of your eye you see that he has reached one of the master control consoles here in the heart of the alien device. The Doctor pulls out his sonic screwdriver.

If one of the warriors sees the Doctor, go to 58. If no one sees the Doctor, go to 15.

5 Martha has pulled you into another airlock. The Doctor tries to shut the inner door behind you but it's firmly stuck.

'Doctor!' Martha bellows and pulls him clear just as a shot rings out. The three of you tumble out of the airlock and on to the surface again. You run and find somewhere to take cover and wait.

And wait. Nothing happens.

'Have they given up?' Martha whispers after a long silence.

'It looks like it,' the Doctor agrees but he is looking very puzzled.

The Doctor suggests that you move away from this airlock and around the perimeter of this wreck. Slowly you creep around the broken freighter. It's unnaturally quiet save for the whisper-like creaking of metal all around you.

Suddenly you turn a corner and find yourselves looking directly at the three warriors.

If the Doctor speaks first, go to 70. If the alien speaks first, go to 68.

6 'My ship may be a battleship but we were on a mission of peace when we were attacked by the cowards who live here,' states the alien, firmly.

'Why cowards?' you ask.

'Only a coward strikes like that; without warning and without ever showing their own face. It was an unprovoked, unjustified and devastating attack launched without any of the protocols of war.' The alien speaks quietly but you can tell that he is seething at what he sees as an injustice.

'My personal guard and I were lucky to escape with our lives.' He looks at you with a look of determination blazing in his eyes.

'I will avenge my fallen men,' he assures you quietly. 'Those responsible for what happened will pay for their cowardice.'

If one of you tries to answer this next, go to 31. If you hear an odd noise, go to 39.

7 **S**uddenly Martha's phone rings and she pulls out her phone.

'It was the Doctor,' she tells you after a brief conversation. 'He says we can turn off the machine for good now.' She shuts her phone.

You pull the switch back to the off position and the alien technology all around you stops working again, this time forever.

'We're to meet him back at the TARDIS,' Martha tells you.

'Couldn't he have brought the TARDIS here?' you wonder.

'Don't expect miracles,' Martha tells you. 'He's a Time Lord not a magician.'

You set off on the long walk back to the TARDIS but Martha is a very fast walker and she's soon some distance ahead.

Suddenly someone grabs you from behind.

If it was an alien who helped you earlier, go to 9. If it was a human who helped you earlier, go to 97.

8 When the smoke clears you can see the three alien warriors are standing in the ragged gap where the door used to be.

'Hello again,' the Doctor says brightly, 'Small world, eh?'

Two of the warriors raise their weapons but the central alien extends an arm to hold their fire. Carefully he removes the catches of his helmet to reveal what looks like a tiger's head.

'Another cat person?' mutters Martha. 'But not from New, New, New, etc Earth this time?'

'No,' the Doctor confesses, 'not this time. But there are countless feline races in the Universe, almost as many as there are human variations.'

'If you've quite finished talking about my genetic heritage, I do have more pressing questions I'd like answered,' the tiger warrior tells you, with a hint of impatience.

If Martha speaks next, go to 31. If you hear an odd noise, go to 39.

9 You struggle and manage to get free. You see that your assailant is the alien Kudir.

'What are you doing?' you ask him. You realise now that he disappeared while you were dealing with shutting down the alien machinery, but you hadn't noticed at the time.

'I thought I might need a hostage,' he tells you, pulling out an energy weapon from inside his clothing. 'No energy-draining machine any more,' he tells you, 'so this is fully functioning.'

Suddenly a shot rings out and the weapon is knocked out of the alien's tentacle.

'Not much good if you can't hold on to it, though, is it?' asks a familiar voice.

You turn round and see the Doctor with Martha and a dozen or so uniformed humans who are clearly police of some kind.

'I took the opportunity to call in some old friends of yours,' the Doctor tells the alien, 'The Inspector here and his team want to ask you a few questions.'

'But what about the medicine?' you ask.

The Doctor explains that there never was any medicine or any plague come to that. The real cargo in the alien's hold is a rare spice called Potsis, used in the finest cuisine. 'I thought I recognised the smell of it when we first arrived,' he reminds you. 'Got quite a sensitive nose, me...'

The Doctor hands the prisoner over to the Space Police team and leaves them to begin the task of repairing and cataloguing the crashed ships.

'Time for us to slip away,' he tells you.

Back in the TARDIS the Doctor is very relieved to be able to resume normal service. He releases the handbrake and the space/time craft launches, immediately hitting turbulence and sending you all flying.

This adventure is over but your journey in time and space continues...

The leading warrior fires his weapon into the air. 'Everyone stand absolutely still,' he orders. He looks around at the alien technology around you. 'Is this the device that is preventing our ship from functioning and draining our power?' he asks the Doctor who nods. 'Turn it off,' he orders. 'That's exactly what I want to do,' the Doctor replies to your surprise.

'But Doctor what about the Black Hole?' asks Martha.

'Your ship carries micron fusion warheads I assume,' states the Doctor, a grim expression on his face.' The warrior nods curtly. 'Then I need you to launch every last one,' the Doctor tells him.

'Are you mad?' he responds, 'You'll destroy us all.'

'Quite the opposite,' the Doctor tells him. 'With that surge of power we can close down that space/time anomaly for good.'

'Are you sure?' you ask.

'Well, pretty sure,' the Doctor confesses, 'but it's the best shot we've got.'

The warrior considers for a moment. 'I can operate my ship's weapon control from here,' he tells the Doctor, ' But only if I have power for my comms device.'

The Doctor holds up his Sonic Screwdriver. 'I might be able to help you with that. Do you trust me?'

The warrior nods and hands over his communicator. The Doctor gives it a quick blast with the screwdriver and hands it back. The soldier prepares the launch signal.

'Ready?'

'Fire!' says the Doctor,

The warrior launches his warheads. As soon as they explode the Doctor activates the alien device. The technology all around you springs into life humming and buzzing. The Doctor operates the controls and fires the collected energy in single pulse directly into the Black Hole.

If the Black Hole disappears go to 37. If nothing seems to happen go to 99.

The Doctor is impressed. 'Wow — take a look at this. This is serious technology!'

'Yeah, but what does it do?' asks Martha.

'I wish I knew,' the Doctor tells her and starts to explore. You and Martha have to run to catch him up as he dives between the various components of the massive machine. 'Most of this stuff is concerned with capturing and storing the energy but I can't work out to what end yet,' the Doctor tells you.

'Maybe this will help,' he speculates, as you reach a central platform. It's home to a gigantic three-dimensional hologram showing the local star system.

'Is that... a black hole?' says Martha, pointing at something in the centre of the display.

'It looks like it but it can't be, that's just impossible. We'd be pulled over the event horizon faster than you can say Raxacoricofallapatorius!'

'And you would be — without the Guardian,' a new voice explains.

You look around and see that a vaguely humanoid robot has joined you.

'What Guardian?' asks Martha.

'This is the Guardian,' the robot indicates the machine around you. 'It's been here for thousands of years protecting this entire sector of space from the black hole.'

'Which explains the constant need for energy,' comments the Doctor.

'I regret the necessity to steal the energy from passing spaceships but it was for the greater good,' confesses the robot.

'But what about the crews of all the crashed ships?' asks Martha.

'We treat all the injured survivors and then long-range teleport them to the nearest inhabited system.'

'But you're not about to do that to us?' the Doctor asks, suspiciously.

'I want you to help me.'

If the Doctor asks what he can do, go to 72. If the warriors arrive, go to 24.

12 The human drains the bottle, leaving a few dregs of water, which he pours on to his face. 'Sorry,' he says eventually, in a voice still croaky with disuse, 'I must be quite a state; a disgrace to the uniform.'

'Imperial Space Marine?' asks the Doctor in a knowing tone.

'Commander Dylun Kesh, at your service,' smiles the survivor. 'How did you...?'

The Doctor nods at the partly ripped badge on his chest. 'Thought I recognised that,' he says modestly.

Martha winks at you. 'He's such an anorak at heart,' she whispers. 'He probably collected stickers of them when he was a kid.'

'I heard that,' replies the Doctor keeping his focus on the Space Marine. 'So Commander, any idea what did this to all these space craft?

'Let me show you,' says the Commander.

If he takes you to a cave, go to 53. If he takes you to a secret bunker, go to 20.

Kesh has adjusted his weapon and thrust it into the control console.

He looks over at you all and explains what he has done. 'I've set the weapons power pack on overload. You'd better take cover. When it goes off in about ten seconds, there's going to be quite a big explosion here.'

He runs towards the doors, but the Doctor tells you to stay where you are.

'But the big explosion?' Martha reminds him.

'Come on, Martha Jones,' says the Doctor. 'You don't believe everything you're told do you?'

You've been counting the seconds down in your head. 'Ten!' you call out and close your eyes. Nothing happens.

When you open your eyes again, the Doctor is grinning.

'Machine that sucks up energy, remember?' says the Doctor.

If the problem is a spaceship, go to 35. If the problem is a planet, go to 67.

'I need someone to take my place,' explains the robot.

'What?' you say in surprise.

'I was created to do a simple job,' the robot continues. 'To keep the machine running, to serve the Shield. But over the years I have grown. I have a lot of time to think... I've begun to dream. Of other planets and new places. I want to travel. I want to see the Universe.'

The robot's electronic voice seems to be on the verge of breaking up with emotion.

'Just like us, Doctor,' whispers Martha in awe. The Doctor just looks at the robot without commenting.

'But I cannot go anywhere unless someone takes care of the Shield. If it fails there will not be anywhere for me to visit.' The robot looks at you. 'Please help me,' it begs.

If an alarm begins to sound, go to 78. If the warriors arrive, go to 4.

The Doctor is making adjustments to the controls with his sonic screwdriver. He glances over his shoulder and shakes his head at you, indicating for you to keep quiet. Unfortunately the movement catches the lead warrior's eye.

'What are you doing?' he demands.

'Trying to save the day,' explains the Doctor, without looking up from what he is doing. 'Now tell me, does your battleship have micron fission warheads?'

The warrior hesitates.

'See that black hole? If I can't get this fixed none of us are going anywhere,' the Doctor says persuasively.

'We do have such devices.'

'Excellent.'

You and Martha are horrified. What's excellent about some kind of bomb?

'Don't get me wrong,' explains the Doctor. 'I despise all weapons, particularly ones of mass destruction...'

The warrior is preparing to fire.

If you throw yourself at his legs, go to 85.
If you call out a warning, go to 69.

The robot takes the Doctor to a central console where a padded chair sits on a raised dais. The Doctor sits and the robot fixes a tight-fitting helmet to his head.

'This may be slightly uncomfortable,' the robot warns the Doctor.

'Long as you don't mess the hair do,' replies the Doctor, with a smile.

Suddenly the Doctor's face contorts with pain.

'Are you all right, Doctor?' Martha calls out.

'Just dandy,' the Doctor manages to say through clenched teeth. 'Whatever that means. Or maybe that should be just Beano. Or Whizzer and Chips.'

'He's babbling,' says the robot.

'He's always like that,' you explain.

'I heard that,' the Doctor tells you, removing the helmet and crossing to a nearby console.

Suddenly you hear heavy footsteps and the aliens you met earlier arrive.

If you call out a warning, go to 69. If they fire a warning shot, go to 10.

'You're making a big mistake,' the Doctor tells Kesh, but the man is not prepared to listen to you.

He points the gun at you and tells you to move away from the controls.

'If you just turn off this machine you'll cause destruction on a massive scale,' the Doctor tells him again. 'Don't do it.'

'I asked you to keep quiet,' the man replies tersely, 'I'll shoot if I have to.'

You and Martha exchange nervous looks.

'Have you got a plan, Doctor?' Martha whispers at him urgently.

The Doctor shakes his head. 'Not as such,' he confesses, 'but I'm working on it.'

'What are you doing?' you ask, looking over at Kesh.

Kesh glances in your direction. 'Turning this thing off,' he tells you, 'permanently.'

If he has a grenade in his hand, go to 90.
If he has done something with his energy weapon, go to 13.

18 You start to walk along the corridor, which is made of metallic rings joined together.

'Why would anyone build something like this just to make spaceships crash?' asks Martha.

'Maybe the answer is at the end of this tunnel,' suggests the Doctor.

'If we ever get there,' you mutter.

The Doctor hops across to a small panel on the wall, smiling to himself. He gives the alien controls a blast of sonic energy and suddenly the floor beneath your feet begins to move. You realise that the wide black rubber carpet running down the middle of the floor is a transportation device. 'I didn't think anyone would build a tunnel like this and expect everyone to walk,' he explains with a grin.

Suddenly the moving pavement stops, hurling the three of you to the floor.

If the lights go out, go to 22. If a sliding door opens, go to 28.

Martha takes a step forward and gasps in amazement.

You and the Doctor hurry to join her. An incredible sight greets your eyes.

'A spaceship graveyard!' the Doctor mutters.

'More like junkyard!' you suggest.

It does look a bit like a junkyard, or perhaps a metal recycling plant, but on a massive scale. Under a cloudless sky the colour of spring grass is a sandy terrain covered, as far as the eye can see, with wrecked spacecraft. There are small ones not much bigger than a large car, medium sized-ones about the size of a large house and some massive ones as big as office blocks but they all, big and small, have one thing in common — they all look as though they crash-landed.

'The power drain that we had in the TARDIS isn't a new thing then,' comments the Doctor looking out over the wrecks.

'Where are all the crews?' you ask. 'Surely there were some survivors from these crashes?'

'Good question,' says the Doctor.

'Maybe they can tell us,' adds Martha pointing towards a particular nearby wreck. The spaceship she is indicating is one of the larger ones – a dark battleship covered with gun turrets and laser blasters. At the rear of the ship a ramp has been extended from an exit and three large humanoid figures are moving down it with determined strides. They have clearly seen you.

'That looks like a military vessel,' you suggest. 'Do you think they'll be friendly?'

'We'll soon find out,' comments the Doctor.

'Are they... Judoon?' asks Martha, remembering her first encounter with aliens.

'No, I don't think so,' replies the Doctor, 'the armour's wrong.'

If you duck back inside the ship, go to 65. If you wait for them to reach you, go to 70.

Your new companion leads you between the hulks towards an area relatively free of wreckage. Here he shows you a low circular structure set into the ground.

'The entrance is through here,' he tells you, indicating a doorway that leads into the building.

Inside you find a spiral staircase, which leads deep into the planet. You begin descending and try to keep count of the number of steps but you lose count somewhere in the five hundreds.

'How far down are we going?' you ask, as your legs begin to ache.

'I think we've had our exercise for the day,' Martha agrees.

'Nearly there,' announces the Doctor, as the staircase finishes in an antechamber leading into some kind of underground building.

You walk through a short corridor and find yourselves in a large hall full of strange machinery and computers. Massive glass columns seem to be full of crackling blue electric fire. The Doctor is excited. 'Now this looks like it means business, doesn't it?' he comments, running around and taking in the various details of the alien machine.

'Over here,' he calls, summoning you to a central console.

You all join him.

'This is the main user interface,' he tells you. 'Let's see if we can get any sense out of it.'

The Doctor uses the sonic screwdriver to activate the equipment and a computer generated animated face appears on a screen above you.

'Defence Status Alpha,' it announces in an electronic voice, 'Containment is standard, energy levels at 70 per cent.'

'Containment of what?' you wonder.

'Containment of the Breach, of course.'

'May we see the Breach?' asks the Doctor. The screen changes to show an image of local space.

If you see another planet, go to 51. If you see a spaceship, go to 93.

You shine the wind-up torches around the room you have now entered. It is oval shaped with a number of workstations around the edge. The Doctor is sniffing the air with a curious expression on his face. 'That smell,' he mutters, 'I'm sure I should know that.' Then he shakes his head and starts examining the Captain's Chair.

'This is a Draconian ship,' he announces, ' so this must be... of course, the "Regal Prince"!'

'Isn't that a curry house in Goodge Street?' asks Martha giving you a cheeky wink.

'Yes it is,' the Doctor nods, pulling the carpet from under Martha's cheekiness,' but it's also the name of a Draconian vessel that went missing in mysterious circumstances,' the Doctor says, smiling broadly, 'like the Marie Celeste or Amelia Earhart...'

If you want to know more about the ship go to 95. If you want to explore more go to 86.

You are plunged into pitch darkness.

'Don't move,' the Doctor tells you, urgently. Moments later, he locates one of the torches you had earlier, which he had put into one of his impossibly large coat pockets.

He shines it around and locates a set of sliding doors in front of you. With his sonic screwdriver he opens them and you are almost blinded by the light within.

'It's a lift,' the Doctor informs you, 'go in.'

After a moment your eyes begin to adjust. You can now see that you are in the largest lift you've ever been in.

The Doctor presses the only control and the doors slide shut. Moments later they begin to open again.

'Have we gone anywhere?' you ask.

'Take a look,' replies the Doctor.

If there is someone waiting for you, go to 61. If there is a massive chamber in front of you, go to 11.

You skid to a halt and are amazed at the sight that greets you.

An alien creature is attacking the Doctor and Martha. The monster is a blue-skinned humanoid with three legs and four arms. The arms end in hand-like appendages covered with tendrils. Two of these arms are holding your friends on top of their heads. It isn't clear if they are in pain or not, but their position does not look comfortable.

'Let them go!' you shout, and begin to look for something you can use as a weapon. You spy a cricket ball-sized rock and bend to pick it up.

'Wait!' calls the Doctor as you pull back your arm ready to throw.

You see that the alien has let both the Doctor and Martha go.

If the alien is the next to speak, go to 76. If Martha is the next to speak, go to 62.

Suddenly there is the sound of heavy boots running and the three battle armour-clad soldiers that you met earlier pour into the room in combat mode. They quickly surround you.

'Hand over the device that crippled our ship,' demands the leader rudely.

'The Guardian is not portable,' the robot informs them.

'Then we want its secrets. We want the technology,' the warrior insists.

You and Martha step forward.

'It's not that simple,' you tell the warrior.

'This whole place is the Guardian,' adds Martha, 'and it's the only thing keeping us from being crushed in a black hole!' she tells them.

The Doctor has quietly crept towards the master control console, which he is now studying carefully. From the corner of your eye you see him pull out his sonic screwdriver.

If one of the warriors spots the Doctor, go to 58. If no one sees the Doctor, go to 15.

You take a step forward and an incredible sight greets your eyes. A vast plain stretches out before you into the distance. The ground itself is covered with spaceships and rockets of all sizes, some as small as a family car, some as large as a twenty-storey tower block. For a moment you wonder if this is some kind of spaceport but then you realise that all of the ships are damaged and show signs of having landed badly. Some are partly buried in the ground at the end of long furrows; others have broken sections or are standing at odd angles.

'Well,' says the Doctor, 'that's what I'd call a Spaceship Graveyard!'

'More like junkyard!' Martha mutters. 'What happened here?'

'At a guess,' begins the Doctor, 'I'd say the power drain that affected us in the TARDIS has been operating for quite a long time.'

'I wonder what happened to the crews?' Martha asks, 'Surely there must have been some survivors from all these crashes?'

You listen carefully but can hear no sound of any other life. In fact the silence is complete save for the occasional creaking of distant wreckage in the light breeze.

And then suddenly something crashes noisily to the ground close by.

'What was that?'

The Doctor has set off to investigate. 'Either this wreck is still settling,' he starts to speculate, 'or we're not alone.' With that, he disappears around the blackened rear of the spaceship. Martha runs after him.

'Come on,' she urges you, 'we don't want to lose him, do we?'

You set off to follow them both and quickly reach the corner they turned.

If you find the Doctor and Martha with an alien survivor, go to 23. If you discover the Doctor and Martha with a human survivor, go to 52.

The Doctor leads the way out of the TARDIS, beckoning to you and Martha to follow him.

The Doctor found you all some powerful torches before you exited the TARDIS and as your beam picks him out in the darkness you find him jumping up and down.

'Nice little planet,' the Doctor tells you. 'Gravity's a little below Earth normal but the atmosphere has enough oxygen for you humans,' he adds. He sniffs the air, curiously. 'I ought to know that smell,' he mutters to himself and then shakes his head, dismissing the thought.

You and Martha shine your torches around. The police box outer shell of the TARDIS, looking dead without its usual glow, stands in the corner of a spaceship's bridge.

'Looks like we weren't the first victims...' announces the Doctor.

If you see something on a wall go to 45. If Martha hears something moving go to 38

'The door held!' you shout out in surprise, but a moment later a painful creaking sound begins to build. The door wobbles and starts to move. In what feels like slow motion, the entire door tumbles forwards and crashes to the floor, revealing the three alien warriors.

'It's just possible,' comments the Doctor with understatement, 'that you may have spoken too soon.'

While two of the warriors cover you with their weapons, the central alien releases the catches of his helmet and removes it. Underneath is something that looks exactly like a tiger's head.

'It's a cat person!' whispers Martha.

'But not like the ones we met in the far future,' the Doctor tells her quietly. 'This is a completely different alien race.'

'If you don't mind, I'd prefer to talk about you,' says the tiger, menacingly.

If Martha speaks next, go to 31. If you hear an odd noise, go to 39.

The sliding doors open to reveal what looks like a large storeroom, the only exit being the door you came through.

'It's a dead end!' you announce, unable to hide your disappointment.

'No, it's not,' Martha tells you. 'I think it might be a lift.'

She points to a gap in the floor at the threshold to the room.

'But it's huge,' you say. 'I've never seen a lift this size.'

'Well, it's not as if they lack energy round here, is it?' mutters the Doctor, stepping into the lift to join you and pressing the single button.

The journey appears to take a matter of seconds.

'Have we really gone anywhere?' you ask the Doctor, as the lift doors begin to open again.

'Take a look,' suggests the Doctor.

If there is someone waiting for you, go to 61. If there is a massive chamber in front of you, go to 11.

Suddenly the Doctor and Martha are pulling you back into the ship. The Doctor uses his sonic screwdriver to close the outer airlock door giving you precious seconds to put some distance between yourselves and the aliens.

After being outside in the light, the darkness comes as a shock and it takes a moment for your eyes to adjust.

'This way,' calls the Doctor and leads you deeper inside the spaceship.

'We may have an advantage,' the Doctor gasps as you run, 'because we have torches and we know the territory.' He stops suddenly and you run into his back.

'Dead end,' announces the Doctor.

'Wait,' you suggest, 'I think I've found another airlock.' You shine your torch beam to show the Doctor and Martha.

'Nice one,' says Martha.

The Doctor leads the way outside.

If the aliens are waiting for you, go to 70. If the coast is clear, go to 57.

The planet hanging in space looks a little like Earth, except for the dominant purple and orange coloured atmosphere.

'Is it inhabited?' you ask.

The Doctor nods and points at some specs orbiting the planet just beyond its atmosphere. 'Satellites and space stations,' he tells you.

'And is that where all this energy is going?' asks Martha.

The Doctor shakes his head. 'Not exactly. But it is being used to protect it. According to these readings there is a massive fault in the time-space continuum close to that planet.'

'Is that bad?' you ask.

'About as bad as it gets. If this machine wasn't keeping the fault at bay it would be a disaster,' the Doctor mutters.

'But this machine is responsible for stealing our power,' Kudir states, 'it has to be switched off.'

If a human led you here, go to 3. If an alien led you here, go to 83.

'Look it's nothing to do with us,' insists Martha bravely. 'We were attacked too,' she adds.

Before the aliens can react, a loud siren goes off and the ground begins to shake. Moments later and a low rumble fills the air. You all stagger as the ground begins to move more noticeably.

'What's happening?' you ask.

'Something's moving below us,' the Doctor answers and you realise that he is right. The solid ground that you were standing on is now revealed to be a pair of camouflaged doors, which are slowly sliding open.

The three aliens have taken defensive positions in the cover of a nearby wreck. They have their weapons pointing in all directions, anticipating a further attack. Meanwhile a platform is rising out of the doorway in the ground. On the platform is some kind of machine, which is topped with a gun barrel wrapped in metallic wiring. The barrel begins to crackle and hiss and bolts of energy dance around it. The power builds and then, suddenly, it explodes out of the barrel and bursts into the sky like a firework.

The Doctor, however, isn't looking up into the sky, he's looking at the platform, which is beginning to retreat underground again. 'Quick!' he suggests. 'Jump on. Let's see where it leads.'

Moments later the doors clang shut again and you, Martha and the Doctor continue to hitch your ride on the descending platform.

'What is this thing?' you ask the Doctor, as you cling on to the alien device.

'The energy that was stolen must be quite volatile,' suggests the Doctor. 'I think this is a safety valve for the excess.'

With a soft bump, the platform stops moving.

If you find chamber full of alien technology, go to 46. If you find a tunnel, go to 18.

'Attack you?' You can't help but sound incredulous in response to the warrior's question. 'Do we look as if we go around attacking great big battleships?'

The warrior slowly moves his head from one side to the other to take a good long look at the three of you.

'You do not look threatening,' he agrees, 'but looks can be deceptive. Something stole our ship's power and caused us to crash here. Somebody must be held responsible.'

'But not us,' the Doctor assures him. 'Trust me, we're not the problem. Tell us what happened to you.'

'My warriors and I were travelling back to the Homeworld,' explains the warrior, 'when we were forced to abandon our planned route due to solar flares. Our detour took us through uncharted territory and then we began to lose power.'

If you hear an odd noise, go to 39. If Martha speaks next, go to 31.

33 Kesh waves the weapon in your direction. 'Keep your hands where I can see them,' he orders you, 'and move away from the controls.'

You hesitate and look towards the Doctor. There is a long pause, then the Doctor nods at you to do as you've been instructed.

'Is there anything I can say to stop you making this mistake?' the Doctor asks Kesh, as you shuffle past him.

'No,' the man replies firmly.

'We can't just let him do this, Doctor,' Martha whispers at him urgently.

The Doctor nods and winks at you both.

'It's quite a delicate piece of technology,' the Doctor tells Kesh. 'Do you really think you can operate it?'

Kesh glances round at you. 'I don't need to,' he tells you.

If he has a grenade in his hand, go to 90.
If he is going to use his energy weapon, go to 13.

You find yourselves in another dark corridor. 'Are you sure this is some kind of spaceship?' you ask the Doctor.

He nods. 'Oh yes... or at least it was. I don't think this has flown anywhere for a very long time.' He stops and sniffs the air, a puzzled look on his face. 'Funny,' he mutters to himself, 'Can you smell anything?'

'No,' Martha shakes her head.

'Well I can, and I should know what it is...' He shakes his head in frustration. 'Never mind. Come on.'

You reach a sliding door, which is stuck halfway open.

'I think we can squeeze through,' announces the Doctor before slipping through then narrow gap.

You let Martha go next and then squeeze through yourself.

You find yourself on the ship's bridge.

If it looks as if it has been ransacked, go to 87. If it looks like a tomb, go to 47.

On the screen the spaceship is still stuck - halfway between hyperspace and normal space.

'What would happen,' you ask in a curious voice, 'if the spaceship completed its move?'

The Doctor spins on his heels and grasps you by the shoulders. 'Of course!' He rushes back to the console.

'But you didn't answer my question,' you complain.

'What happens is what always happens when a ship jumps into hyperspace... the hole in space-time seals itself up... which is just what we want to happen.'

The Doctor finishes making some adjustments to the controls with his sonic screwdriver.

'Right then, this is going to be tricky,' he tells you. 'I need to get across to that spaceship and fix the problem at the source but to do that I need the TARDIS to work properly. But in order for that to happen...'

'The machine here has to be turned off,' Martha finishes for him.

'But that's just what we don't want to do,' you point out.

The Doctor nods. 'So, here's the plan,' he tells you. 'We're going to shut off the machine here for exactly thirty seconds, which will give me the time to do my galactic AA man routine. Now I reckon it will take me about thirty minutes to get back to the TARDIS, so use Martha's watch and time me. On that mark pull this lever to zero and count thirty seconds, then return the lever to the original position.'

The Doctor checks you understand what you have to do and then sets off.

The half an hour passes in no time and on Martha's signal you turn off the machine. Anxiously you watch the spaceship on the screen.

If the spaceship disappears, go to 73. If nothing happens, go to 42.

'Get your head down,' the Doctor calls as shots ring out and bullets bounce off the ceiling above you. Martha and the Doctor dive into one doorway and you dive in the other direction.

'Meet us at the surface,' mouths the Doctor and disappears. You realise that you are in the corridor that leads directly back to the point where you entered the alien base. The Doctor and Martha must think that they can find another route and you trust them to do it.

There are no further gunshots but you know that whoever (or whatever) shot at you, must still be around and you keep moving as fast as you can.

Finally you see sky and realise that you've reached the surface. You step out on to the sandy ground and suddenly — someone grabs you from behind.

If you met an alien earlier, go to 9. If you met a human earlier, go to 97.

'Yes,' shouts the Doctor, slapping the leader of the soldiers on the back. 'We did it.'

'But what happened?' you ask.

'Well, it wasn't really a black hole,' explains the Doctor, 'it was a sort of ... rip in the fabric of the universe. It just needed a huge influx of energy to repair itself.'

The warriors promise to fix the robot and help him salvage as many of the ships as possible.

'Will you stay and help?' asks the robot.

The Doctor looks a little embarrassed. 'Love to,' he begins ' but I really have to get this young human home in time for tea, or I really will be in trouble.'

He takes you and Martha back to the TARDIS.

'Do I really have to go home straight away?' you ask.

The Doctor grins. 'Let's just see, shall we?' he suggests and starts up the engines.

The End.

'I think it was down here,' Martha says, leading you along a spaceship corridor.

'I can't hear anything,' you tell her.

'Neither can I now, but I did hear something,' she insists.

The Doctor suggests that you stand still and listen for a moment.

'A ship this size is never entirely silent even when empty,' he tells you.

You cast your torchlight around and spot something scrawled on a wall. 'Look, someone's tried to leave a message,' you call out.

The three of you play your combined torch beams over the alien script, which is made up of squiggles and dots.

'I thought the TARDIS translated language for us?' you ask the Doctor.

The Doctor looks a little sad. 'Not without power,' he mutters, popping his glasses on to study the writing more closely.

If the Doctor can read the message, go to 88. If he can't read the message, go to 94.

Suddenly the air is filled with a piercing siren. Moments later the ground begins to shake and a low rumble fills the air. All of you lose your footing.

'Is it an earthquake?' you wonder.

'I don't think so,' the Doctor answers and as if to mock his words the ground beneath your feet begins to move. You realise that you are standing on a pair of camouflaged doors set into the ground, which are sliding open.

The three warriors have reacted to the siren as befits trained soldiers. They've retreated to the cover of a nearby wreck and taken up defensive positions. When the doors have fully opened a blast of purple energy explodes out of the hole.

The Doctor, however, isn't looking up into the sky, he's looking down to see what else is beneath the ground. 'Look!' he shouts at you. 'There's a staircase inside. Let's see where it leads.'

You, Martha and the Doctor begin walking down the staircase, which spirals around the deep shaft. Above you, the doors clang shut again.

'What about the warriors?' asks Martha, as some angry and loud banging on the doors from above echoes down the shaft.

'Probably for the best that they stay on the surface,' mutters the Doctor, his voice wafting up to you from below. 'I want to find out what's happening here and I fear our soldier friends might prefer to shoot first and ask questions later.'

'Talking about questions — what do you think just happened?' you ask the Doctor, as you continue your descent.

'I think it might be a safety valve for the excess energy that was stolen,' he explains.

You reach the bottom of the staircase.

If you find a chamber full of alien technology, go to 46. If you find a tunnel, go to 18.

Martha continues to read the Captain's log entries.

'This is worse than reading my sister's diary. Every day is pretty much the same,' she complains.

'Try the last entry,' suggests the Doctor.

Martha flicks through and reads the last incomplete entry.

'He must have been in here, off duty, when it all kicked off,' she announces. 'One minute he's moaning about the slow progress because of a meteorite storm and then it's all happening – sudden power loss and people disappearing...'

'Why didn't any of us disappear?' you ask.

'Good question,' the Doctor tells you. 'To go with all the others we're collecting. Time to get some answers, I think,' he declares.

'We need to get outside this ship to find out what's going on.'

After a short search you find an airlock.

If the Doctor leads the way, go to 54. If Martha leads the way, go to 19.

41 The Doctor locates the manual override for the powerless airlock controls and opens the outer doors. Martha gasps in amazement at the sight that greets her as she steps up to join you at the threshold.

Under a pale sky the colour of weak custard is an endless plain, covered with the broken remains of hundreds and hundreds of spaceships. It looks like a scrapyard or a dump. There are spaceships of all shapes and sizes. Some look like little fighter craft, others are more like space-going container trucks. The wrecks stretch out all around you as far as you can see.

'A Spaceship Graveyard,' gasps Martha.

'You can say that again,' comments the Doctor, as he too joins you on the threshold. 'Whatever it is that attacked the TARDIS has been doing this to other ships and, by the looks of things, it's been doing it for quite some time.'

'Where are all the people?' you ask and then correct yourself. 'Or aliens? Or whatever? These ships must have had crews.'

Martha spots some smoke rising from behind a wreck a short distance away.

'Maybe whoever lit that fire can tell us,' she suggests.

You set off to investigate the smoke and discover that beneath the carpet of broken spacecraft the plain is rather hilly, and the walk is very tiring. Some of the wrecks are quite large and it is impossible to keep the plume of smoke in constant sight.

'Are we there yet?' you ask as the Doctor disappears around a corner.

'I think we might be,' the Doctor's voice carries back to you. You turn the corner.

If you find the Doctor and Martha with an alien survivor, go to 23. If you discover the Doctor and Martha with a human survivor, go to 52.

You watch the screen intently but nothing seems to be happening.

'Twenty-eight, twenty-nine, thirty,' announces Martha who has been timing the thirty seconds. 'Time's up.'

'But nothing's happened,' you complain. 'Maybe the Doctor needs more time.'

Martha looks at you sternly. 'He made us promise not to leave the machine off for longer than thirty seconds, we have to have faith in him,' she reminds you.

You push the lever back to its original position and the alien machinery all around you hums back into life.

On the screen the spaceship suddenly disappears.

Delighted, you and Martha jump up, cheer and high-five each other.

'So, what happens now?' you wonder. 'The Doctor didn't go into much detail about that.'

'He rarely does,' Martha says with a grin.

If the Doctor speaks to you by radio, go to 92.
If Martha's mobile begins to ring, go to 7.

43 The Doctor takes hold of the Log and starts speed-reading, flicking through the pages as if they contained a flick-book animation rather than words.

'This is why I stopped using a diary,' he tells you. 'Too much like hard work.'

'How does the story end?' you ask the Doctor.

The Doctor completes his reading.

'The Captain must have been in here, off duty, when it all started,' he tells you. 'One minute he's complaining about problems with the engines and then it all starts happening — just like in the TARDIS — a sudden power loss. And then people start disappearing...'

'None of us disappeared!' you point out.

'Good point,' the Doctor replies. 'We need to get outside this ship to find out what's going on,' he declares.

After a short search you find an airlock

If the Doctor leads the way, go to 54. If you lead the way, go to 25.

44 You and Martha follow the Doctor into a semicircular room full of workstations surrounding a central command chair. The Doctor uses his sonic screwdriver to activate the log computer sited in the Captain's chair.

'We were right. This is a Terran ship on a freight run... so this must be... of course, Sector 42...'

'Sector 42? What's that?' you and Martha chorus.

'An urban myth, a mystery,' the Doctor says, smiling broadly. 'Like the Bermuda Triangle on Earth and baggage reclaim at Heathrow Terminal Three... it's a place where things go missing in mysterious circumstances...'

'Things like people's suitcases?' you query, puzzled.

'At Heathrow yes, but here it's more spaceships that go missing. They call it the Spaceship Graveyard.'

You hear distant sounds of movement.

If Martha thinks she knows where the sound came from, go to 38. If no one is sure where it came from, go to 74.

45 | You find some writing scrawled on a surface.

'Someone's tried to leave a message,' you announce. The Doctor and Martha join you and play their own torchlight over the panel you've discovered.

The writing is in some alien alphabet — all squiggles and dots. Martha can't read it either.

'I thought the TARDIS translated language for us?' she asks the Doctor.

The Doctor nods. 'Unfortunately the TARDIS can't do very much without power.'

You sigh heavily. 'So this isn't going to help us then,' you complain.

'Luckily, I've got quite a knack with languages,' he tells you, proudly.

'Good at everything, this one,' comments Martha, with a friendly nudge.

'Okay then, Doctor, what does it say?'

The Doctor pops his dark-rimmed spectacles onto his nose and studies the strange writing carefully.

If the Doctor can read the message, go to 89. If he can't read the message, go to 94.

46 | The chamber you find yourselves in is full of advanced alien technology. You and Martha can't begin to make sense of it but the Doctor looks fascinated.

'What is it?' you ask him but he doesn't answer immediately.

'Don't worry,' Martha tells you. 'He's having a geek moment. He'll put his glasses on in a minute, you watch.'

'I heard that,' mutters the Doctor shooting a glare at Martha. He is now wearing his glasses which causes both you and Martha to laugh.

'So what's the diagnosis, Doctor?' Martha asks, still giggling.

'This is just some kind of substation,' the Doctor tells you. 'We need to get to the heart of this complex.'

'And how do we do that?'

The Doctor opens a door to reveal a long tunnel. 'We walk!'

If you find a lift, go to 48. If a sliding door opens, go to 28.

47 | You expect a spaceship bridge to look smart and efficient but instead what you're looking at is cold and dead. There is a thick coating of dust covering all the odd bits of equipment at all the workstations that are placed around the rim of the oval-shaped bridge.

'How Clean is Your Spaceship?' jokes Martha.

The Doctor has found a metal plate fixed to the wall. 'This looks interesting,' he mutters, and produces a yellow duster from one of his coat pockets. A moment or two later he has wiped the thick layer of dust clear from the plate to reveal a schematic map of the spaceship. The Doctor traces a path to the main airlock with his finger.

'Let's take a look outside,' he suggests and leads you the airlock he identified on the map.

If Martha leads the way out, go to 19. If you go first, go to 25.

48 The Doctor uses the sonic screwdriver to open the lift doors.

'Is there anything that can't do?' you ask, amazed at the versatility of the pen-like device.

'It's not much cop at peeling apples,' confesses the Doctor. 'Or at getting stones out of horses' hooves,' he adds.

Martha nudges you. 'Luckily we don't do a lot of that,' she tells you as you enter the lift.

The Doctor presses the single button on the control panel and the doors close. Seconds later they begin to open again.

You turn to the Doctor and complain. 'It didn't work,' you tell him but he just shakes his head gently.

'Take a look,' he suggests, nodding over your shoulder.

You turn around and look out of the now open lift doors.

If there is someone waiting for you, go to 61. If there is a massive chamber in front of you, go to 11.

Suddenly, and without warning, the man throws the bottle at Martha, who is knocked to the ground. The man takes off but the Doctor runs after him.

'Just another difficult patient,' Martha mutters as you help her to her feet.

You see that the Doctor has already caught up with the man.

'It's alright, we're not going to hurt you,' he tells him, earnestly.

This time the man takes the water when it's offered to him. After he has drained the bottle he seems to calm down.

The Doctor explains how you came to be here and the man nods — the same thing happened to him.

'I'm just sorry I couldn't stop it,' he tells you.

The Doctor is interested. 'You know what did this?' he asks.

'Let me show you,' says the survivor.

If he takes you to a cave, go to 53. If he takes you to a bunker, go to 20.

Once the Doctor has cranked the door open, you go out and find yourselves in a vast warehouse.

Before you left the TARDIS, the Doctor gave you and Martha powerful wind-up torches which you now use to illuminate the huge room you've emerged into.

'At a guess, I'd say this was a space freighter's hold — but on the ground, not in space,' the Doctor comments, examining the contents of the nearest box. 'Hmm tea,' he announces.

'Tea?'

The Doctor turns to you and smiles. 'English Breakfast Tea to be precise. One of five great unique Earth food exports into the Universe, along with chocolate fingers, chicken tikka masala, chips and, er... something I can't remember. And there's something here else, too... A smell I should know. It'll come to me... Right then, shall we explore?'

If you find the freighter's control room, go to 44. If you find the captain's cabin, go to 84.

On the screen you can see a planet that looks a little similar to Earth.

'Is it inhabited?'

'According to this it's called Ursooma, population eighty billion.'

'And what has Ursooma got to do with all this?' asks Martha waving a hand at the alien technology that surrounds you on all sides.

'This,' the Doctor states simply and points at an area close to the planet. At first you cannot see anything different about it but then you see that there is something there, like a double image.

'What is it?'

'Some kind of fault in space-time... and this machine is all that's stopping it from destroying this entire system.'

But your new companion isn't convinced. 'We can't leave here while this machine is running,' he insists. 'It has to be switched off.'

If a human led you here, go to 3. If an alien led you here, go to 83.

52

The human survivor is dressed in ragged clothing that might once have been a spacesuit and has a long and unkempt beard. His face is dirty and, as you come closer, you realise that he doesn't smell very pleasant either.

'It's alright,' the Doctor is assuring him, holding his hands out palm first in the intergalactic gesture of peace, 'we're all in the same boat.'

'B-boat?' mutters the man, with some difficulty. His voice sounds croaky as if he hasn't spoken for a long time. 'Couldn't launch lifeboats... no power...'

Martha steps forward and produces a bottle of water from her bag, 'Here drink this,' she says, handing the bottle to him. He looks at it suspiciously.

'It's okay,' she tells him, 'you can trust me. I'm a doctor. Well, almost!'

If the man turns aggressive, go to 49. If he starts to become friendly, go to 12.

Your new friend leads you through the maze of broken spaceships towards some hills. As you get higher up, the number of wrecks decreases, allowing you a better view of your surroundings.

'Why have all the ships landed here?' you wonder. 'It's a big planet.'

'That's a very good question,' the Doctor tells you.

Kudir leads you into a dark cave mouth.

'Don't worry,' he assures you, 'there is light.'

You walk down a short passageway and find the rocky walls give way to smoother, metal walls that suggest a building of some kind. Soon you emerge into a well-lit room the size of a concert hall packed with alien machinery. Large metallic coils run from the floor to the high ceiling in groups of seven, all crackling with sparks of blue electricity.

'Is this where the energy went?' asks Martha.

The Doctor nods. 'But what for, that's what I need to know.' He finds a computer console and, with a quick blast of his sonic screwdriver, persuades it to cooperate. Page after page of information scrolls over the screens.

You watch in amazement as the Doctor speed-reads the data as it whizzes before his eyes.

'Oh this is bad, this is very bad...' he mutters.

'Care to share?' asks Martha, raising an eyebrow.

'You were right,' the Doctor tells him, 'some of the stolen energy is here, but most of it is being sent out here.'

He activates a control and a screen comes to life showing an image of local space.

If you see another planet, go to 30. If you see a crippled spaceship, go to 91.

As you cautiously stand on the threshold of the airlock, the Doctor steps up beside you and announces that there is a breathable atmosphere and that it is safe. You and Martha hurry to join him and you are both stunned at the sight that greets you.

At first it makes no sense — it looks like a scrap metal yard or a municipal dump or perhaps a metal recycling plant. Under a brooding sky the colour of a bad bruise is a rocky terrain, liberally sprinkled with thousands of broken spaceships and rockets.

'A spaceship graveyard!' you mutter in awe.

The Doctor agrees. 'Whatever it is that attacked the TARDIS has been doing this to other ships and, by the looks of things, its been doing it for quite some time.'

Some of the spaceships are quite small, possibly single-person fighter craft, whilst others are massive; space-faring luxury liners and container ships. There are countless dead spaceships of every size, colour and design imaginable.

'Where are all the people?' Martha asks. 'These ships must have had crews.'

'Good question,' the Doctor says.

'Well there are some over there,' you tell them pointing in the direction of a nearby hulk — a gun-grey battleship bristling with weaponry. Three figures can be seen in a doorway. They seem to be humanoid and dressed in heavy battle armour or spacesuits. As you see them, they see you and begin to move towards you.

'Do you think they're friendly?' asks Martha, a little nervously. 'That ship looks military to me.'

'We'll soon find out,' comments the Doctor.

'Do you recognise them?' you ask.

'At first I thought they might be Sontarans.'

'Or Judoon?' speculates Martha.

'No, no, the armour's wrong.'

If you duck back inside the ship, go to 29. If you wait for them to reach you, go to 68.

55 You feel as if your lungs are going to explode. You've never run as fast or as far.

'Not much further,' the Doctor tells you from a few metres ahead. Annoyingly he doesn't seem to be having any trouble breathing. He doesn't even appear to be sweating.

You stop running and lean against a fairly undamaged fighter craft. Martha comes back to you. 'You need to be fit if you want to travel with us, you know,' she tells you, with a wink. 'Come on!'

She hurries on while you stop and catch your breath for a moment. You lean over with your hands on your knees. After a moment or two you stand up again and suddenly someone — or something — grabs you.

If you met an alien earlier, go to 9. If you met a human earlier, go to 97.

The Doctor tells the alien creature that he understands his desperation. 'But we cannot allow the lasting damage that will be caused if this machine is turned off.'

'But what about the medical supplies?' wails the alien, 'I cannot afford to lose any more time.'

'If we can find a solution I can get your supplies to your people in no time at all,' the Doctor assures him, 'And I promise you that's what I will do.'

'Our... er... spaceship is very fast,' you assure the alien.

The alien doesn't look very convinced.

'But while this machine is still working no one's spacecraft will be going anywhere, so it's all academic.'

'Oh I don't know about that,' says the Doctor, taking another look at the various controls on the alien machine's consoles.

If the problem is a planet, go to 67. If the problem is a spaceship, go to 35.

57 You find yourselves back on the planet's surface, outside the ship in which the TARDIS materialized.

There is no sign of the aliens, nor of their ship, as you are further around the wreck. You can now see that there is a slight pattern to the crashes. There seems to be more wrecks closer to a point some miles away, where some kind of tower can be seen rising high above the spaceship graveyard.

The Doctor has seen it too.

'Looks like a likely place to get some answers, what do you reckon?' he says.

'Looks miles away,' complains Martha.

'Then we'd better start walking then,' replies the Doctor, cheerfully.

You turn a corner and find yourselves face to face with the aliens again. You raise your hands in surrender.

If the aliens speak first, go to 68. If the Doctor speaks first, go to 70.

'Step away from there,' orders the soldier.

The Doctor doesn't even turn his head. He continues to scan the controls.

'I'm sorry I can't do that,' he replies, 'Slight case of the end of the Universe to deal with. Now tell me, is your battleship carrying micron fission warheads?'

The warrior hesitates.

'End of the Universe remember?' repeats the Doctor urgently.

'Yes,' the warrior finally tells him, 'there are such devices on my ship.'

'Good.'

You and Martha exchange a shocked look. You can't believe the Doctor is pleased about that.

'Now I hate any weapon,' explains the Doctor, 'especially one as dirty, powerful and indiscriminate as yours but I have to acknowledge that they are huge potential sources of energy so...'

You see that the warrior is preparing to fire.

If you throw yourself at his legs go to 85. If you call out a warning go to 69.

'Weren't you listening?' you demand of the alien Kudir, outraged at his suggestion. 'If we turn off the alien machine it will be a disaster.'

The Doctor agrees. 'We have to find another way,' he insists.

The alien stands in his way and suddenly produces a weapon.

'I'm sorry,' he says, 'but it is imperative that I get home. My ship is carrying emergency medical supplies. There is a plague ravishing my home planet and the cargo in my ship could save millions of lives. But time is of the essence.'

'You have enough medicine in your ship to save that many people?' asks Martha, incredulously.

'A tiny dose of the medicine is all that is needed for each person. If they get the treatment in the first three days of illness.'

If Martha promises to help him, go to 82. If the Doctor has an offer, go to 56.

60 | Once the door is open, the only thing you discover about where you've landed is that it's dark.

'Wait here,' the Doctor orders you and disappears back inside the TARDIS. Using his sonic screwdriver as a torch he locates an emergency supplies cupboard and extracts three compact torches.

As he hands one to you, he tells you that the torches are hand-powered.

'With a bit of luck the energy level will be low enough not to attract the attention of whatever it is that stole our power.'

'Where are we?' asks Martha, taking her own torch and beginning to wind it up.

'In a spaceship — but one on the surface of the planet we saw, not in space,' the Doctor tells you.

With your torches on full power you step out of the TARDIS.

If you've landed on a spaceship's bridge, go to 21. If you're in a spaceship's hold, go to 80.

The figure before you is vaguely human-shaped but instead of legs it has a single spherical foot/leg. Its body is also spherical but packed with articulated arms of various sizes, with different implements at the end of each one. The robot's "head" has been designed to look like a human face; with eyes and a mouth in the right place and two ear-like protuberances each side of the head.

'Please come this way,' he asks you.

The robot takes you into the heart of the control system and shows you a screen. On it is an image of outer space and a strange anomaly, a swirling mass of light.

'Is that a black hole?'

The Doctor nods. 'It looks like one but if that was really a black hole this planet and everything around it would have been pulled inside it centuries ago.'

'Not while I am here,' the robot tells you. 'And not while the Shield holds.'

'What Shield?' asks Martha.

The robot opens its arms wide. 'This is the Shield. This entire complex was created to protect this sector of space from the black hole.'

'But that must take an enormous amount of energy...' the Doctor mutters, thinking it through. He snaps his fingers suddenly. 'Of course, that's the reason for the energy drain. The Shield takes energy to maintain itself.'

The robot nods. 'At first it took energy from passing comets and meteors but it wasn't enough. So spaceships became our next targets.'

'But what about the crews?' asks Martha.

'We do not mean to harm anyone. Every survivor is kept in suspended animation.'

'But why haven't you frozen us?' the Doctor asks, suspiciously.

'I believe you may be able to help me.'

If the Doctor asks what he can do, go to 14. If the warriors arrive, go to 78.

'It's okay,' Martha tells you with a smile, 'he wasn't hurting us.'

'I needed to access your language,' explains the alien in a quavering voice, 'I hope my telepathic contact was not... uncomfortable.'

Martha brushes a hand through her hair, which is a bit of a mess now. 'Nothing a comb wouldn't fix,' she mutters.

'I am Kudir,' the alien tells you, 'from the Kropil system. My ship crashed here four days ago.'

The Doctor nods. 'Of course, I should have known,' he tells you. 'The merchants of Kropil are well known travellers and explorers.' He asks Kudir if he has any ideas about what has made all these spaceships lose power and crash on this particular planet.

Kudir tells you that he's discovered something that might give you some answers and offers to show you.

If he takes you to a cave, go to 53. If he takes you to a bunker, go to 20.

In response the engines fire up again, but at an even higher pitch. Martha flicks a quick look of alarm in your direction. She's never heard the TARDIS in this state before either.

'Something on that planet below is draining our power,' explains the Doctor. 'Which is impossible,' he adds, looking perplexed.

'There's only one thing we can do — emergency landing and try and find the source of the problem.'

The Doctor turns his attention back to the controls, the emergency red lighting casting   deep shadows in his suddenly serious face.

Martha reaches out to you and gives your arm a reassuring squeeze. 'Don't look so worried,' she tells you.

With a sudden crunch and a loud bang, the engine sounds die away.

If the Doctor thinks he has enough residual power to open the doors, go to 26. If the Doctor needs to use a crank handle to open the door, go to 50.

You quickly hurry through some doorways and bulkheads trying to put as much distance as possible between you and the aliens.

Your eyes have now adjusted to the light of the outside world and you find it difficult at first to cope with the darkness again. Your flashlight begins to falter and you have to frantically wind the crank to generate some more power.

The Doctor sees that you are in trouble and uses the sonic screwdriver to activate a door control. A solid metal door falls into position, cutting you off from the aliens.

Martha is grateful of the chance to catch her breath.

Suddenly the door the Doctor closed begins to shake. Black smoke begins to trickle from the edge and then there is an explosion, which knocks you all to your feet.

If the door has been blown open, go to 8.
If the door is intact, go to 27.

You duck back inside the ship and race through the double doors of the airlock, switching your torches on as you go.

'Which way?' you ask.

'This way,' reply the Doctor and Martha simultaneously. Unfortunately they are both pointing different directions.

Martha suggests you go with the Doctor but as you set off your foot catches on the corner of a step and you go flying into Martha, knocking you both to the floor.

'Come on,' mutters the Doctor, 'this is no time for dancing.'

You can hear heavy footsteps, suggesting that the aliens are following you.

'I'm hoping we'll have the advantage because we have torches,' the Doctor tells you as he helps you to your feet, but a moment later a harsh white beam of light suddenly fills the room.

If you let the Doctor pull you one way, go to 64. If you let Martha pull you away, go to 5.

The room is a sort of lounge. There are a number of comfortable chairs and low tables. In one area there are some benches and long tables, and the remains of a meal can be seen on numerous plates. The food is half-eaten.

'Looks like they left in a hurry,' comments Martha.

'Actually it's even odder than that,' adds the Doctor, pointing at the chairs by the unfinished meals.

'They didn't finish eating, that's what I meant,' Martha says, frowning.

'But look at the chairs,' the Doctor insists. 'If they had left in a hurry, some kind of panic, the chairs would be all over the place, but they're not.'

Meanwhile you have found another set of important-looking doors.

You suggest to the Doctor that you explore whatever is behind them.

If the Doctor tells you to go first, go to 54.
If you let the Doctor go first, go to 34.

The Doctor is looking at the screen showing the planet again, searching for a solution.

'We can't turn this off if it means all those people die,' says Martha in a horrified whisper.

You stare at the odd part of space near the planet that contains the fault in space/time.

'If that wasn't there,' you say, 'then this machine wouldn't be necessary.'

'Brilliant,' says the Doctor, patting you on the back.

'So how do we do it?' Martha asks, practical as ever. 'How do you heal a rip in space/time?'

'Find a space/time Doctor?' you suggest.

'We've got one of those,' Martha reminds you.

The Doctor is clicking his fingers. 'Yes, yes, yes, good thinking,' he says, pointing at you.

'What did I say?' you ask. The Doctor starts running between various consoles that control the alien machine, blasting them with his sonic screwdriver.

'Your medical analogy is spot on,' he tells you. 'The anomaly is like a wound, like a scraped knee and it needs to heal. But at the moment all this,' he waves a hand at the alien machine, 'is just protecting it.'

'Like a great big plaster?' you ask.

The Doctor nods. 'But the plaster is too tight. It's not allowing the wound to heal.'

'So what's the answer?' asks Martha.

'I remove the shield and let the energy pour into the wound where it can be used to heal it.' The Doctor stands back and gives the controls one last blast with the sonic screwdriver. 'I've given us about thirty minutes. When this all goes off we have to be back in the TARDIS.'

'Or what?'

'You don't want to know.'

If you get back to the surface without seeing anyone, go to 55. If you get shot at, go to 36.

'You will obey every minute detail of our instructions 0if you wish to survive,' announces the lead alien. 'Our translation software has scanned and acquired your language. There should be no excuse for any misunderstanding,' he adds, in his strangely musical voice.

'Couldn't agree more,' replies the Doctor, cheerfully. 'Although sometimes it's the non-verbal language that speaks more than words.' He nods at the two warriors who are pointing their rifles at you. 'Is it really necessary to hold us at gunpoint? We're not armed.'

The alien considers this for a moment and then nods at his companions, who lower their weapons.

The lead alien removes his helmet, revealing a craggy, wrinkle-skinned humanoid with odd tufts of hair sprouting from his face, like grass on a rocky surface. Deep set solid blue eyes regard you all carefully.

If you speak next, go to 81. If the alien speaks next, go to 6.

'Doctor, look out!' you cry.

The lead soldier glares at you. 'Restrain the child,' he orders his guards and they grab hold of your arms.

'Leave him alone!' shouts Martha, pulling at one of them.

'I'm asking you to trust me,' the Doctor tells them. 'I need to set off every warhead on your ship.'

'You'll destroy this planet,' replies the warrior.

'The Guardian will soak up the energy a split-second after the explosions and we can use it to put a seal over that black hole,' the Doctor replies.

'Are you sure?' asks Martha.

'Well, you could always cross your fingers,' suggests the Doctor and he presses the final switch.

There is the momentary sound of a massive explosion and then nothing. Suddenly all the machinery around bursts into activity, a deafening hum builds in the air and then, with a sudden pop, everything returns to normal.

'Yes!' shouts the Doctor. 'We did it.'

The warriors are looking around in amazement. On the screen the black hole has disappeared. The Doctor grins.

'It was really a tear in the fabric of space/time,' explains the Doctor, 'not really a black hole in the classic sense. And with enough energy it would heal itself, like our own bodies heal if we're injured.'

The Doctor goes over to the warriors and explains what has happened. They are grateful to the Doctor for freeing them and offer to help the robot with clearing up. 'And when you're ready to leave,' adds the Doctor, 'perhaps you can take the robot here with you. He'd like to explore the Universe.'

When you, Martha and the Doctor get back to the TARDIS, some hours later, it is back to normal and ready to launch.

This adventure is over but where will the TARDIS take you next?

70 'We're unarmed,' the Doctor tells them, 'you don't need to point those weapons at us.'

'I'll be the judge of that,' replies the central warrior, removing his helmet. Underneath you are surprised to discover that it isn't an alien at all. It appears to be a heavily battle-scarred human with a patch over one eye.

'You're human?' you say in surprise.

'Terran born and bred,' he assures you.

'At least we can understand you,' comments Martha. 'Perhaps we can help each other.'

'That depends,' the warrior tells you, 'on how much you are prepared to cooperate.'

'Oh we're very big on cooperation,' the Doctor assures him. 'We love the Co-Op. Not to mention Sainsburys, Tescos, Morrisons...'

'I don't know what you're babbling about,' complains the soldier. 'Just answer me this — why and how did you attack my ship?

If you answer him, go to 32. If the Doctor answers him, go to 75.

You step out into a spaceship corridor that is both dark and very, very cold. Your foot slips and you realise that there is frost on the floor.

'Be careful,' warns the Doctor, but he's too late and you've already fallen on your bottom and skidded a couple of metres in an undignified manner. Martha tries very hard not to laugh at you but only succeeds in losing her own balance. Soon the Doctor is also on the floor.

'Now you know why I wear this big coat,' he tells you, laughing. 'It's padding for occasions like this!'

Carefully, the three of you get to your feet and start exploring again.

You reach a pair of large sliding doors, which the Doctor tries to open.

'Give me a hand — they've been iced shut.'

If you've found the bridge of this ship, go to 21. If you've found a mess room, go to 66.

'I need to be replaced,' explains the robot.

'What?'

'My sole function is to maintain the Guardian,' explains the robot. 'But I have served for a thousand years and my circuits are beginning to corrode, my mobility is restricted, and I believe my efficiency will soon be compromised.'

'You need a holiday, mate,' says Martha. 'You're suffering from stress.'

The Doctor smiles. 'I think this is more than a medical problem,' he tells you.

'But if I left here the Guardian might fail,' says the robot, in a concerned voice.

The robot looks at you. 'Please, you have to help me,' it begs.

The Doctor sighs. 'I don't think we can take your place,' he tells the robot, 'but there might be another answer. I'll need access to the system computers.'

If the robot allows him access, go to 16. If the robot cannot give access, go to 2.

As you watch the screen, the spaceship suddenly disappears,

Martha is counting off the seconds.

'Twenty-eight, twenty-nine, thirty. Okay, put the lever back up.'

You try to push the lever back to its original position but it's stiff and refuses to move.

'Help me,' you cry and Martha runs across to assist. With the two of you throwing your weight at it, the lever finally begins to move.

You both let go of the lever and wipe your brows, relieved.

'I hope it wasn't off for too long,' you mutter, exhausted by the effort.

Martha has another concern. 'I'm more worried about the Doctor,' she confesses. 'He didn't allow himself much time, did he?

You tell Martha you're sure the Doctor knows what he is doing. And cross your fingers for luck.

If the Doctor speaks to you by radio, go to 92. If Martha's mobile begins to ring, go to 7.

All is silent again now.

'Perhaps we imagined it,' Martha wonders as you continue to search for the source of the sound.

'No,' the Doctor tells her, 'there was definitely something.'

'Could it have been wind, or something natural?' you speculate, hopefully.

'It's possible,' the Doctor agrees, 'But not very likely. If this ship crashed recently you might expect to hear sounds of it settling, but from the looks of things, this ship crashed a long time ago.'

You reach a set of impressive-looking double doors. They appear to be locked but the Doctor manages to loosen them with his sonic screwdriver. He starts to pull the doors open.

'You can help you know,' he mutters. You and Martha hurry to help, pushing and pulling at the doors to part them.

If you find have entered another corridor, go to 84. If you find yourselves outside the ship, go to 25.

'Babbling? Me?' the Doctor says, sounding mortally offended. 'I don't do babbling. Blathering sometimes, waffling even on the odd occasion, but never babbling.'

'Enough!' orders the warrior in a voice that would stop a tank. 'Just tell me how you got here.'

'I suspect our story is similar to yours,' the Doctor tells him. 'Our ship lost power and we crashed.'

The soldier nods. 'That's pretty much how it happened for us. We were on our way home from the Front, looking for some R and R. We've been on combat status for eighteen months, we weren't looking for any trouble.'

'But trouble found you,' says the Doctor, sympathetically.

'It just hit us out of the blue. We had no time to react. It's a miracle that the three of us survived the impact.'

If you hear an odd noise, go to 39. If Martha decides to reply, go to 31.

'Now I can speak your language,' the alien explains.

Martha puts a hand through her hair and pulls a face as she finds some sticky residue in it. 'What did you do?' she demands.

'I am sorry if my physical contact caused discomfort,' the alien tells you.

'Nothing like a touch of alien sweat hair gel, I always say,' says the Doctor brightly.

The alien explains to you that he is from a race of merchant travellers from a planet called Kropil. 'My name is Kudir, and by the protocols of the Imperial Code I demand that you release my ship.'

The Doctor informs him that you've only just arrived yourselves and don't know what attacked your ships.

Kudir tells you he's found something that might explain it and offers to show you.

If he takes you to a cave, go to 53. If he takes you to a bunker, go to 20.

You walk through the darkened corridors of the space freighter.

'It's odd, isn't it, that the cargo is still intact?' you comment, as you follow the Doctor and Martha.

'How do you mean?' Martha asks you.

'Well,' you continue, following the thought through, 'If someone made this ship crash you'd have thought they would have taken the cargo, wouldn't you?'

'Smart thinking,' the Doctor commends you and winks at Martha, 'I told you this one was smart, didn't I?'

You reach a set of impressive-looking double doors. The Doctor tries to open them but they are heavy and stiff. He looks at you and Martha and raises an eyebrow. 'You could try and help rather than just stand there and watch!' he suggests.

Soon you have the doors open.

If you have found the ship's bridge, go to 21. If you find yourselves outside the ship, go to 19.

An alarm sounds and you hear heavy running footsteps. Before you can even think about hiding, the three warriors you met earlier have surrounded you.

'No more games,' the leader shouts, waving his space rifle aggressively. 'I want the power draining device and I want it now.'

The robot turns to the newcomers and addresses them. 'Have you come to take my burden?' he asks them hopefully. 'I am tired and I would like to see something of the universe before my circuits succumb to entropy.'

'Where is the device?' the leader of the warriors asks again, aggressively.

'You are in the Shield now,' the robot answers helpfully. 'It is all around you.'

The Doctor carefully takes his sonic screwdriver and takes aim at some controls.

If one of the warriors sees him, go to 58. If the alien notices, go to 15.

'**W**hat's happening?' asks Martha, nervously.

'Something is draining our power,' answers the Doctor. 'Something on the nearest planet.'

'How is that possible?' you ask him.

'I don't know,' confesses the Doctor. 'But we will have to make an emergency rematerialisation and then try and find the source of the problem.'

The Doctor turns his attention back to the controls. The red emergency lights cast deep shadows across the entire control room making it feel like a haunted house.

Suddenly there is a large bang and sparks shoot out from the console as if a firework has gone off. Then there is silence.

'We're here,' announces the Doctor after a moment. 'Shall we find out where here is?'

If the Doctor uses the sonic screwdriver to open the doors, go to 96. If the Doctor uses a crank handle to open the doors, go to 60.

'It's big,' announces the Doctor, 'Whatever it is.' You wave your torch beams around to try and work out what kind of space this is. You see piles of packing crates and containers.

'This is the hold of a space freighter,' the Doctor tells you with authority. 'Circa the middle of the twenty —fourth century.'

'Wow, you can tell all that just by looking?' you ask him.

Martha coughs and points to a large label on the nearest container. It reads

> **From:** Terran Moonbase Spaceport
> **To:** Hydra Three
> **Despatch:** 10/10/ 2356

'He's good but he's not that good,' she tells you trying not to laugh.

The Doctor sniffs the air and frowns. 'I must be losing my touch. I should recognise that smell.'

He shakes his head and suggests that you explore further.

If you find yourselves in a corridor go 77. If you find the captain's cabin go to 84.

81 | '**I** think we might be in the same boat,' you tell the alien.

'I do not understand,' he replies.

'We were travelling and lost all power to my, er ... spaceship,' the Doctor explains.

The alien nods.

'Then we may indeed be fellow victims,' he agrees. 'My men and I were conducting a diplomatic mission, one that might finally have stopped this endless war we've been fighting since my father was a boy, but now we will never know if we would have been successful.'

'Maybe there is a way off this planet,' the Doctor tells him.

'Maybe there is, if we can find the cowards who put us here.'

'Why cowards?' you ask.

The warrior turns to look directly at you.

'Only a coward strikes without warning,' he tells you gravely.

If Martha responds to this, go to 31. If you are interrupted by a sudden noise, go to 39.

'We can help you, I promise,' Martha tells the alien. She looks at the Doctor. 'We can, can't we?'

The Doctor hesitates and scratches the back of his ear. 'Well... in theory, yes, of course. The TARDIS can get that medicine to where it's needed in next to no time.'

'You see, I told you,' Martha tells Kudir enthusiastically.

'But that does rather require the TARDIS to be functioning... and this machine to be turned off,' continues the Doctor glumly.

The alien nods his head in agreement. 'As I said, the machine has to be switched off.'

You cannot believe what you are hearing.

'Are you seriously going to just shut this thing down?' you demand.

The Doctor flashes you a quick grin. 'Of course, but not before I've solved the problem here.'

If the problem involves a planet, go to 67. If the problem involves a spaceship, go to 35.

Martha is shocked at the alien's statement.

'Don't you care about all the lives that will be lost if this machine is turned off?' she asks him furiously.

'Of course I don't want to cause more death and destruction but if I don't get home with my cargo in the next few days it will be too late for my people,' the alien tells you, his tentacles quivering with emotion.

The Doctor is intrigued. 'What do you mean?' he asks.

'There is a plague on my home planet, thousands have already died and many millions, maybe billions more are at risk. But there is a cure. And the hold of my ship is packed full of the medicine.'

He sounds quite desperate, but very sincere and Martha is clearly convinced by his words.

If Martha promises to help him, go to 82. If the Doctor has an offer, go to 56.

You follow the Doctor down a dark corridor. It's spooky and cold. The ceiling is dotted with light panels that are not working and each door you pass is frozen in a semi-open position.

'This may tell us something,' announces the Doctor stepping through a doorway, 'it's the Captain's cabin.'

Inside Martha finds a log book on the Captain's desk. 'I thought Captain's Logs were like computer blogs not handwritten diaries,' she complains, flicking through the pages.

'There's a big retro thing going on in this time period... old is the new new as it were,' explains the Doctor.

'You're right, Doctor,' Martha tells him. 'This was a cargo freighter. Do you think it was attacked by pirates?'

'Pirates wouldn't have taken the crew and left the cargo,' mutters the Doctor.

If the Doctor takes the Log to study, go to 43. If Martha carries on reading, go to 40.

You hurl yourself at the warrior's legs, knocking him off balance. His shot goes wild into the high ceiling. The other two warriors turn their weapons on you.

'Leave him alone!' shouts Martha rushing to join you.

Meanwhile, the robot has rolled over to the Doctor.

'What are you doing?' he asks.

'Remotely setting off every warhead in the crashed battleship!' answers the Doctor pressing a sequence of switches. 'Cover your ears and close your eyes,' he adds as a warning seconds before a huge distant explosion rocks the entire base.

'Doctor — what about the radiation?!' Martha can't believe what he has done but the machinery around you is suddenly pulsing with life as lights flash and dials spin.

'Trust the Shield,' shouts the Doctor and returns to the controls. Moments later there is a massive flash of light and suddenly all the machinery around you stops working. The lights fade back to normal.

'Yes,' shouts the Doctor punching the air.

The warriors are looking around in confusion. On the screen the black hole has disappeared. The Doctor grins.

'You see it wasn't really a black hole,' the Doctor explains, 'it was a tear in the fabric of the Universe. It just needed a huge influx of energy to repair itself.'

The Doctor goes over to the warriors and explains what he has done. The leader thanks him for freeing his ship and the three soldiers salute him and then leave.

The robot tells you that he will begin to revive the crews held in suspended animation.

'I'm sure one of them will take you exploring,' the Doctor says.

You, Martha and the Doctor make your way back to the TARDIS, which is now restored to full health.

This adventure in time and space is over, but where will the TARDIS take you next?

86 You and Martha lead the way back into the dark interior of the ship.

'I think we should look for an airlock and try and get out of this ship,' the Doctor suggests. 'Whatever it was that caused us to lose power isn't going to be found in here.'

The Doctor thinks that he can remember the layout of this kind of ship.

'It's been a while,' he confesses, 'and I looked much older when I was younger, 'he adds confusingly, 'but if I'm right, and I usually am...'

'Except when he's not,' mutters Martha in a whisper. The Doctor shoots her a look and continues. 'There should be an airlock about here...'

You turn a corner and find the airlock staring you in the face.

The Doctor shines his torch onto his face and beams.

If the doors are closed, go to 41. If the doors are open, go to 25.

The bridge is semi-circular in shape and features a handful of workstations around the perimeter, all facing a large viewscreen. At least that's what the layout suggests but all the equipment to make this a fully functioning starship bridge is missing.

Martha flicks her torch beam around the scene of destruction.

'Looks like the day after a closing down sale at Dixons,' she suggests.

'Someone's taken every piece of high technology,' the Doctor says.

'But why?' Martha asks, 'What's the point if there's no power here?'

'Perhaps someone found a way to overcome the power drain,' the Doctor replies, thinking aloud. He rummages in the debris and locates a schematic diagram which shows the layout of the ship.

'The main airlock is near here,' he says pointing at the map. 'Let's take a look outside.'

If the doors are closed, go to 41. If the doors are open, go to 19.

88 'There's something about it being a regular shift and then this "suddenly my colleagues are gone. They've all disappeared."'reads the Doctor.

'What does he mean — "disappeared"?' asks Martha.

The Doctors studies the alien script again, his eyes narrowing with concentration.

'I may have the translation wrong,' he confesses. 'It's a fiddly language, especially in its written form. If you don't dot your gerks and cross your bas, it's almost impossible to read at all!'

The Doctor slips his glasses back into his jacket pocket and gets to his feet.

'Right,' he announces with purpose. 'We've got plenty of questions, let's start getting some answers.'

You show him the airlock you've found.

'After you then,' suggests the Doctor, 'since you found it...'

If you go agree to go through the airlock first, go to 41. If you would prefer the Doctor to go first, go to 54.

'It's an account of what happened,' announces the Doctor, concentrating on the alien message. 'This is an Hyanthorg ship, a race of peaceful explorers, from the so-called Twelfth Galaxy.'

'Why is it the so-called Twelfth Galaxy?' you ask, intrigued.

'Numbering something like a galaxy is always a difficult thing,' he explains with a grin. 'It all depends on where you start you see. I know of at least three Galaxy Fives in different parts of the Universe. It makes map-making almost impossib-' the Doctor's voice trails off mid-word.

'What is it?' asks Martha.

'Our blogger just stops,' says the Doctor, 'but the last thing he writes is that his fellow crewmen just start to disappear.'

You find a door that appears to lead to an airlock and call the Doctor.

If the Doctor tells you more, go to 88. If he decides you should explore through the airlock, go to 41.

As you watch in horror the man pulls out a small pineapple-shaped object. 'Grade 3 Accelerator Grenade,' he tells you, as he presses a control on it. 'Looks pretty innocent, doesn't it? But it'll take out all of this in a split-second.'

He begins to run.

'If I were you, I'd find some cover,' he yells as he dashes past, 'you've got twenty seconds...'

You turn and start to follow him but the Doctor calls you back.

'We haven't got time for that,' he tells you.

'Twenty seconds,' you remind him.

The Doctor just walks up to the console where the grenade is sitting.

Martha is timing the twenty seconds with her watch.

'Nineteen, twenty! Close your eyes!' she calls but nothing happens.

The Doctor indicates the alien technology around you. 'Great big energy vacuum, remember?'

If the problem is a spaceship, go to 35. If the problem is a planet, go to 67.

'What is it?' you ask.

The Doctor shrugs. 'Some kind of freighter, I think. But it's been there a very long time.'

'Looks abandoned,' suggests Martha. 'No lights on, no one at home...'

The Doctor nods solemnly. 'If it wasn't for this machine here, it would have broken up years ago.'

He consults the readouts in front of him and his face is grave, as the flickering lights play over his features. 'It looks like it had some kind of problem coming out of hyperspace,' he tells you.

'But is this machine responsible for sucking the energy out of our spaceships?' asks your new friend.

The Doctor nods. 'And it's using that energy to hold that ship in stasis.'

'Then we must shut it down!'

If a human led you here, go to 3. If an alien led you here, go to 83.

A speaker set into one of the consoles crackles into life and a familiar voice can be heard.

'Hello, hello, this is DJ Doc with a shout out to my posse. Are you there?'

You shoot a puzzled look at Martha who just shrugs.

'I think he's at a funny age,' she tells you, 'apparently the late nine-hundred's can be an odd time for his kind. He says its his forty-second childhood.'

The Doctor tells you that he's landed back where you first landed and suggests that you join him. First, he suggests that its safe to turn off the machine for good.

On the way back to the TARDIS, you find yourself falling behind Martha. You call after her but suddenly someone or something grabs you from behind.

If it was an alien who helped you earlier, go to 9. If it was a human who helped you earlier, go to 97.

The spaceship looks very old. The hull is pitted with dents caused by passing space debris. It seems to be glowing with red glitter.

'What's wrong with it?'

The Doctor studies the readouts on the consoles in front of him.

'It's had an accident — a bad one,' he tells you. 'It looks like it suffered some kind of complete systems failure at a very bad time — in the instant of moving from hyperspace back into real space time.'

'So it's stuck in a sort of inter-dimensional doorway?' asks Martha.

'Exactly,' the Doctor nods, 'but the problem with a hyperspace drive is that it makes it's own doorway... and if that doorway isn't shut the hole in space-time becomes very unstable.

'We have to switch this machine off,' says your helpful guide who led you here.

If he is an alien go to 59. If he is human go to 98

The Doctor gets to his feet and slips his glasses back inside his jacket pocket.

'Right then,' he announces, 'clearly that's not going to give us any answers. Time for Plan B.' He looks at you both hopefully. 'Anyone got a plan B? I'll take a plan C or D at a push!'

Martha has an idea. 'If this ship is another victim of the power drain that affected the TARDIS...' The Doctor nods encouragingly and she continues. 'Maybe we need to look outside this ship.'

The Doctor considers for a moment and then claps his hands. 'Excellent. Brilliant. Very bright girl, our Martha,' he tells you. 'Going to be a doctor, you know.'

'One day,' she agrees.

The Doctor grins. 'Come on, let's find an exterior door.'

You find an airlock.

If the Doctor decides to go first, go to 41.
If Martha decides to go first, go to 19.

95 'The Draconians and the Terrans were on the verge of war,' the Doctor tells you, 'but a faction within the Draconian royal family was determined to make one last attempt to negotiate a settlement with the Earth Empire rather than fight.'

'What happened when the ship disappeared then?' Martha asks. 'Did it cause an interstellar incident?'

The Doctor smiles. 'Actually, it did the reverse. Earth Empire forces worked with Draconians on a Search and Rescue mission and that cooperation laid the ground for a peace accord that lasted nearly two hundred years. The irony was that the Regal Prince did more for peace by disappearing than it could ever have achieved by completing its mission!'

The Doctor suggests that you look for an airlock and leave this ship.

When you find an airlock, if the Doctor goes first, go to 41. If you go first, go to 25.

With the door open you look out to try and see where it is you've landed but it's impossible because there is no light.

'I can't see a thing,' you complain.

'Let's see if I can do anything about that,' says the Doctor.

He steps back towards the raised central area of the control room, using his sonic screwdriver's blue light as a torch. He opens up a box hidden under one of the seats and pulls out two compact wind-up torches.

'I knew these would come in handy one day,' comments the Doctor as he gives you one.

'So where do you think we are?' asks Martha, as she winds up her torch.

'Down on the surface of the planet,' the Doctor tells her, 'but inside another spacecraft. I wonder why it's so dark...'

If the Doctor leads the way, go to 71. If Martha leads the way, go to 34.

You manage to put up a fight and wriggle free from your captor. You are surprised to see that it is the Space Marine Kesh. In the excitement of dealing with the alien machine you had completely forgotten about his hurried escape earlier.

'What are you doing?' you demand, angrily.

'Looking for some leverage, kid,' he tells you, 'don't take it personally,' He makes another grab for you but you're ready for it this time and scramble clear. He begins to chase you but you set off at a high speed, weaving and bobbing through the sea of wreckage.

Suddenly you hear a friendly voice. 'This way,' calls the Doctor.

You look up and see the Doctor and Martha standing on the wing of a nearby wreck.

You clamber up to join them. They reach down to help you up.

Behind you Kesh arrives but before he can begin to follow you he is surrounded by a half a dozen battle-suited marines.

'I ran into some old mates of yours,' the Doctor tells him, 'They seemed quite keen to catch up with you.'

It's not long before you are back in the TARDIS, and on your travels again.

'Our friend Kesh was AWOL from the Space Marines when he went missing,' the Doctor explains when you ask, 'He stole some rather valuable gems from a diplomatic mission, a theft that almost caused a war. Luckily I have a very sensitive nose.'

'How does your nose come into it?' you ask.

'For long haul security jewellery in this age is packed in an organic jelly — a jelly which has a very distinctive aroma,' the Doctor tells you, 'that's what I smelt when we first left the TARDIS.'

This adventure is over but your journey in time and space continues...

Martha is scandalised.

'Didn't you hear a word the Doctor said?' she asks the man, who introduced himself as Commander Dylon Kesh. 'If this machine stops working it will be a complete disaster. Millions and millions of people will die.'

The man shrugs. 'Millions of aliens,' he tells you. 'There are no human colonies in this sector of space,'

A dark look appears on the Doctor's face.

'Are you really suggesting that millions of aliens dying in a flood of raw destruction is a price worth paying for our freedom?' he asks in a low voice.

Kesh looks embarrassed. 'When you put it like that? No, of course not. But what choice do we have?'

'There has to be another way,' the Doctor tells him. Dylon shakes his head and points a weapon at you all.

If he speaks next, go to 33. If the Doctor speaks next, go to 17.

'Nothing's happening,' you complain.

'Give it time,' the Doctor whispers and then suddenly there's a huge flash of light and the black hole disappears.

Everyone cheers.

The Doctor explains that it wasn't really a black hole at all. 'It was a tear in the fabric of the universe. It just needed repairing.'

The warriors tell you that they will fix the robot and then stay on the planet to help him salvage as many of the crashed ships as possible.

'Will you stay too?' asks the leading warrior.

The Doctor shuffles and looks at his feet, 'Sorry, but I have to get this young human home or I really will be in trouble.'

You say your goodbyes and head back to the TARDIS. Inside you ask if you really have to go straight home. The Doctor grins and operates the launch controls.

'Let's just see, shall we?' he suggests.

This adventure is over but your journey in time and space is over...